Disney
FROZEN

MELTING HEARTS

Disney PRESS

LOS ANGELES • NEW YORK

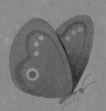

Written by Suzanne Francis
Illustrated by the Disney Storybook Art Team
ISBN 978-1-4847-4773-5
F383-2370-2-15195
Printed in China
First Edition, September 2015
1 3 5 7 9 10 8 6 4 2
For more Disney Press fun, visit www.disneybooks.com

It was a beautiful spring day. The sun was shining over Arendelle as Anna bounced around the kitchen. She had planned a picnic for all her best friends and couldn't wait to get started.

"Are you ready?" Elsa asked, peeking into the kitchen.

"Almost." Anna closed the lid to the picnic basket. "Most of the bags are in the hall, but can you grab that brown one?"

"What's in here?" Elsa asked.

"Just a few picnic essentials," Anna answered.

"You sure you have everything?" Kristoff joked when he arrived a few minutes later. "Maybe you want to bring the stove or perhaps . . . the castle?"

Elsa and Kristoff chuckled.

"I just want everything to be perfect," Anna said.

"It'll be great," Elsa said. "Because we'll all be together."

"I'm already having fun," said Kristoff.

Anna smiled as she struggled with the bags.

"Sven and I can handle those," Kristoff said, taking them from her.

"Hi, everybody!" Olaf shouted as he ran toward his friends. "Oooh. Is that a real picnic basket? I love picnics. I'm so excited. Let's go, let's go, let's go!"

"Let the picnic officially begin," Anna said, leading the way toward the mountains.

Anna took a deep breath. "Those spring flowers make the air smell so sweet."

"They really do," said Elsa.

"Mmmmm!" Olaf said as he sniffed a patch of flowers.

"Hey, look!" Olaf plucked a petal from one of the flowers. "It looks like a heart."

"Wow," Anna said, eyeing the petal. "How pretty!"

As they continued to walk, something caught Anna's eye. She scooped up a leaf and showed it off. "I found a heart, too!"

"Nice," said Elsa. Then *she* began searching.

"Found one!" Elsa called. She held up a smooth heart-shaped stone.

"I bet I can find one," Kristoff said.

"Not before I find another." Anna grinned and raced ahead, looking for more.

Kristoff found a curved twig and bent it into the shape of a heart. "Got one!" he said happily. But then the twig snapped in half!

Even Sven played the game.

As the friends walked on, they continued to search for hearts.

Some looked like broken hearts.

Others looked like perfect hearts.

And a few . . . didn't look much like hearts at all.

But all of them were fun to find!

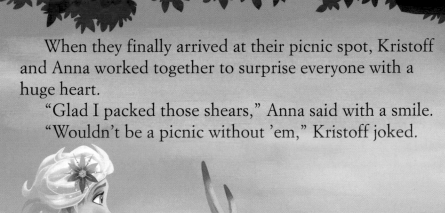

When they finally arrived at their picnic spot, Kristoff and Anna worked together to surprise everyone with a huge heart.

"Glad I packed those shears," Anna said with a smile.

"Wouldn't be a picnic without 'em," Kristoff joked.

Setting the shears aside, Anna took out the blanket.
"This is the best picnic ever!" Olaf shouted as he
helped to spread it out.

Anna began to unpack the bags. . . . It took a while.

"Oh, no!" Anna cried as she dug through the picnic basket. She had forgotten to pack the food!

Elsa couldn't believe it. "You packed candlesticks but no food?"

Anna slowly nodded her head.

Everyone burst out laughing—including Anna.

"Oh . . . but I did remember dessert." Anna happily pulled out a small box and opened it.

"Uh-oh." Anna's smile faded. Her dessert was a melted mess. "They *were* special chocolates."

Just then, it started to rain. "Oh, come on!" Anna
shouted at the sky.

"What a wonderfully refreshing picnic shower!"
Olaf said brightly.

The rain came down harder. "Quick! Under the
blanket!" Anna said.

The group huddled together, trying to stay dry. "Olaf, it's not supposed to rain on picnics," Anna said. "But maybe it should." Olaf smiled. "The rain is keeping us close. It's like a big cuddly hug!"

Drip. Drip. Drip. The rain started to leak through the blanket.

Anna groaned. This was not the perfect picnic she had pictured. "I'm sorry everybody," she said. "Should we just go home?"

"The picnic's not over," Elsa said. She waved her hands and an ice canopy appeared.

"Beautiful!" Olaf said.

"And practical," Kristoff added.

"Thanks, Elsa." Anna hugged her sister. "Maybe we can eat the melted chocolate . . . I'm sure I brought spoons."

Elsa thought for a moment then magically created an ice mold. "Put the chocolate into this . . ."

It worked! They now had heart-shaped frozen chocolate treats!

The friends sat together, eating their treats and watching the rain.

Everyone agreed with Olaf: it *was* the best picnic ever!